Kwanzaa

A Level Two Reader

By M. C. Johnston

The **Child's World**®

Kwanzaa is a holiday that began in 1966. It honors black families and good values.

A man named Dr. Karenga created Kwanzaa. He wanted a special time for black people to think about their history and beliefs.

Kwanzaa lasts for seven days. It begins on December 26 and ends on January 1. On each day there is a different idea to think about.

Candles are important during Kwanzaa. They stand in a holder called a kinara.

On the first night of Kwanzaa, one candle is lit. On the second night, two candles are lit. By the last night of Kwanzaa, all seven candles are lit.

A place mat is used during Kwanzaa. The kinara sits on top of it.

Fruits, vegetables, and nuts are set out during Kwanzaa. They stand for crops people gathered long ago.

Corn is also set out during Kwanzaa. There is one ear of corn for each child in the family.

During Kwanzaa, a special cup is used. It helps people think about family members and being together.

There is a big dinner at the end of Kwanzaa. People give gifts, too. Happy Kwanzaa!

Index

To Find Out More

Books

Hoyt-Goldsmith, Diane. *Celebrating Kwanzaa.* New York: Holiday House, 1994.

Jones, Amy Robin. *Kwanzaa.* Chanhassen, Minn.: Child's World, 2001.

Pinkney, Andrea Davis et al. *Seven Candles for Kwanzaa.* New York: Dial Books for Young Readers, 1993.

Web Sites

Kids Domain
http://www.kidsdomain.com/holiday/kwanzaa/
An explanation of Kwanzaa and lots of fun activities.

The Official Kwanzaa Web Site
http://www.OfficialKwanzaaWebsite.org/
The official site to help you learn more about Kwanzaa.

Note to Parents and Educators

Welcome to Wonder Books®! These books provide text at three different levels for beginning readers to practice and strengthen their reading skills. Additionally, the use of nonfiction text provides readers the valuable opportunity to *read to learn*, not just to learn to read.

These leveled readers allow children to choose books at their level of reading confidence and performance. Nonfiction Level One books offer beginning readers simple language, word choice, and sentence structure as well as a word list. Nonfiction Level Two books feature slightly more difficult vocabulary, longer sentences, and longer total text. In the back of each Nonfiction Level Two book are an index and a list of books and Web sites for finding out more information. Nonfiction Level Three books continue to extend word choice and length of text. In the back of each Nonfiction Level Three book are a glossary, an index, and a list of books and Web sites for further research.

State and national standards in reading and language arts emphasize using nonfiction at all levels of reading development. Wonder Books® fill the historical void in nonfiction material for primary grade readers with the additional benefit of a leveled text.

About the Author

M. C. Johnston started her career as a book editor and designer. Since then, she has written many books for young children. She currently lives in Minnesota.

Published by The Child's World®, Inc.

PO Box 326
Chanhassen, MN 55317-0326
800-599-READ
www.childsworld.com

Special thanks to Stephanie Davenport, Chawah Levi, and the Cummings family
for allowing us to photograph your celebration.

Photo Credits
© Romie Flanagan: cover, 2, 6, 9, 10, 13, 14, 17, 18, 21
© 2002 University of Sankore Press: 5

Project Coordination: Editorial Directions, Inc.
Photo Research: Alice K. Flanagan

Library of Congress Cataloging-in-Publication Data
Johnston, M. C., 1973-
Kwanzaa / by M.C. Johnston.
     p. cm. -- (Wonder books)
"A Level Two Reader."
Includes index.
Summary: A brief introduction to the holiday of Kwanzaa.
ISBN 1-56766-025-8 (lib. bdg. : alk. paper)
1. Kwanzaa—Juvenile literature.
2. Afro-Americans—Social life and customs—Juvenile literature.
3. United States—Social life and customs—Juvenile literature.
[1. Kwanzaa. 2. Holidays.]
I. Title. II. Wonder books (Chanhassen, Minn.)
GT4403 .J67 2002
394.261—dc21
                    2001007942